How Animals Behave

Animal Societies

Jeremy Cherfas

Lerner Publications Company
Minneapolis

Contents

Introduction   3

1   **Groups and Societies**   4
    Looking at Societies   5

2   **Colonies**   7
    A Coral Colony   7
    The Portuguese Man-of-War   8

3   **Social Insects**   9
    An Ant's Life   10
    Workers on a Production Line   11
    Social Signals   12
    Where Did Insect Societies Come From?   13

4   **Birds of a Feather**   14
    Safety in a Group   15
    Exchanging Information   16
    Real Societies   16
    Nesting Together   18
    Competition in the Nest   18

5   **Mammal Societies**   20
    Friendly Vampires   21
    Mongoose Packs   22
    The Family That Preys Together   23
    Hunting   25

6   **Primates**   26
    Baboons of Ethiopia   28
    Ape Societies   29

Glossary   31
Index   31

Introduction

Most people do not like being alone. We like to be with our families and friends. Humans are social animals, and we see that other animals also live in groups. There are schools of fish, swarms of bees, and herds of antelope. We might think that most animals are social, but actually, they are not.

Most of the world's animals live alone. From time to time, they might come together with others like themselves to eat or to breed, but then they go their separate ways. We seldom notice these solitary animals, because most of the world's animals are smaller than we are. We notice the animals that are closer to our size, and many larger animals do live in groups.

If most animals live alone, there must be good reasons why some live together. Food is one reason. Animals that live together may help each other find food. Protection is another reason. Animals in a group can help protect each other from danger. Breeding is also a good reason. Living in a group may help an animal find a mate and raise its young. There are different ways that some animals live together in societies.

A huge flock of snow geese in the southwestern part of the United States. These large birds spend the summer months in northern Canada and move southward in flocks as winter sets in.

Shetland ponies from the Shetland Islands in Scotland. Shetland ponies are strong and live in groups.

1 / Groups and Societies

Some animals live in groups. In a group, roles of individual members are not clearly defined. A school of fish, for example, does not have a leader. Any fish may swim at the head of the school, and as the school swirls around in the water, different fish take the lead. Living with other animals in a group is not the same as being a member of an animal society.

A school of black-spotted grunt. These fish live in small schools and are found in southeast Asia.

Below: Olive baboons are found in central Africa. In a baboon troop, parents are strict with their young.

Societies are more complex than groups. They have rules about how to behave and who may do what. Members of an animal society communicate with each other. They also may receive benefits, such as more food, by being part of a society.

A troop of baboons is not like a school of fish. Baboons live in a society. In a troop, different baboons have different ways of behaving. Females with young babies are in the middle of the group, and all the other baboons are interested in them and their babies. Older infants are allowed to play roughly, although mature baboons may not. Young males stay outside the crowd, often sitting and keeping a lookout. Older males rule the troop and go where they please and do what they like. Each baboon seems to know what it should do, and there are seldom any upsets. Very occasionally, one animal breaks the rules.

A young male may challenge an older male to a fight. If the young male wins, he rules the troop. If the older one wins, he will probably force the younger one to leave the troop. Either way, the baboons soon settle down again.

Looking at Societies

Humans have a difficult time understanding how animal societies work. Part of the problem is that we live in our own human societies, so we think of the animals as if they were humans. For example, when young male baboons sit on the edge of the troop and keep a lookout, they are often the first to spot a leopard and raise the alarm. You may think they are guards. However, the young male may be sitting on the edge because the older males will threaten him if he comes any closer. Perhaps he is looking out for the older males, so he can stay out of their way. While he is on the edge and looking around, he may be the first to see a leopard creeping up. He would become scared and scream an alarm.

This baboon has found a good place to sit and watch for enemies.

Below: A large troop of 30 or more olive baboons, including about 10 young.

Is that young male acting as a lookout? Or does he just happen to see danger while he is sitting apart from the troop? These are difficult questions, even for scientists who have spent their lives trying to understand animal societies. These scientists want to know why animals behave the way they do, and very often they have no simple answer. Just remember that when someone says an animal is a lookout, for example, that does not mean that the animal considers itself to be a lookout. A human just thinks the animal is a lookout.

In the early days of its life, a baby baboon clings to its mother. This baby seems blissfully happy, but the mother is watching out for danger.

2 / Colonies

A Coral Colony

Some animals have no choice but to live together. They are literally stuck in a group. Corals are such animals. Some corals live alone, but most, especially those that build tropical reefs, such as the Great Barrier Reef, form colonies.

The **colony** consists of millions of tiny animals, called polyps, all joined together. Each animal is shaped like a tube, with an opening on one end. The opening, which serves both as a mouth and as a way to excrete waste, is surrounded by **tentacles**. The coral colony grows by budding. One polyp develops a small swelling, which grows until it becomes a new polyp with its own mouth and tentacles.

In a coral colony, all the polyps are identical and all behave in exactly the same way. Other relatives of the coral also form colonies, but different polyps in those colonies do different jobs.

Above: A cup coral is killing a fish. Cup corals live alone or in small groups. Most corals live in colonies in warm waters. The best known are the corals that have built the Great Barrier Reef off the northeast coast of Australia. The red coral, left, is an example of how a coral colony grows by budding. It is found around Japan and in the Mediterranean Sea. The red coral is frequently used for making jewelry.

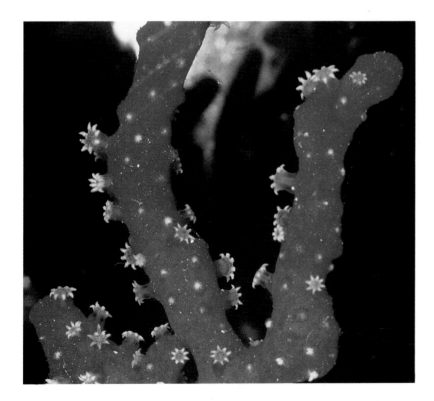

The Portuguese Man-of-War

One relative of the corals is the colony called a Portuguese man-of-war. This colony floats in the water like a jellyfish. It is a complicated colony made up of many individuals.

The colony floats at the surface of the sea, kept up by a gas-filled balloon that catches the wind and acts as a sail. The balloon, which can be 1 foot long (about 30 centimeters), is made up of one kind of animal. Below the balloon stretch tentacles 10 to 100 feet long (about 3 to 30 meters). These tentacles are covered with cells that sting other animals when they come into contact. This sting is so powerful that it can **paralyze** human swimmers who could then drown. No wonder most people leave the beach when the wind blows a Portuguese man-of-war onto the shore.

Along with the balloon and the tentacles, there are stomach polyps. These colony members eat and digest the small fish caught by the tentacles. The food from the stomach polyps nourishes the whole colony. There are also colony members that do nothing but produce eggs or sperm.

Colonial animals that make up corals and the Portuguese man-of-war show no signs that they are aware of the other members of the colony. However, they do have different members doing different jobs, which is called division of labor. Insects also have division of labor and behave much more as we might expect a society to behave.

A Portuguese man-of-war eating a fish it has caught. The gas-filled balloon is at the top of the picture. The stomach polyps and the hunter tentacles hang down below.

Portuguese man-of-war colonies float freely and often wash ashore on beaches. They sting and can hurt humans.

3 / Social Insects

Insects have some of the most complex societies in the animal world. A hive of honeybees might contain tens of thousands of individual female workers, all with their own jobs to do and all working to produce honey. Some build cells in the honeycomb, others look after the growing **larvae**. Some bees fetch food for the whole hive, others guard the entrance to the hive. There are even bees who keep the hive cool by using their wings to fan a breeze. Each bee colony also contains a few male bees, called drones.

Three kinds of insects have societies: (1) ants, (2) wasps and bees (which are closely related to each other), and (3) termites and aphids. There are also solitary **species** in these categories, but the truly social insects have three things in common:

- The mother has help in raising her young.
- Some of the workers never breed.
- The adults live a long time, so that the mother, her grown-up offspring, and her young offspring may all live together.

Not all termites of the same species look alike. A colony includes soldier termites with strong jaws for driving off invaders. The soldiers gather together whenever there is danger. The different kinds of termites found in a colony are called castes.

Aphids are tiny insects that feed on leaves and plant stems, by sucking juices from the plants. They can cause great damage to farm crops and in gardens by weakening plants.

An Ant's Life

The red ant that is common in woodlands, farms, and backyards in Europe is called *Myrmica rubra*. A new society of these ants starts in the late summer, when males with wings and queen females with wings crawl out of the underground nests. They mate, and the male of each pair flies away and dies. The female, however, rubs her wings off, then digs a hole underground or in a tree stump. The queen ant spends the winter there, and in the spring, she lays her first eggs. The eggs hatch into grubs that grow into adult workers, the ants you see scurrying around. All the queen's workers are females, but none of them can lay eggs. They help the queen raise more daughters, most of which will be workers, while a few will be queens.

Red ant workers collect honeydew from aphids. Aphids suck liquid from plants, and ants "milk" the aphids without hurting them.

The iridescent ants of western Australia shine purple or blue in the light. All ant species are social. They work together to find food.

Until her first eggs become adult ants, the queen feeds herself and her offspring on food reserves she stored away while she lived in her own mother's nest. Once her young are fully grown, they become workers and go out looking for food, which they bring back to the nest for the queen and her newest offspring.

Each worker lives a few months, but new generations continue to help the queen raise her offspring for 9 to 10 years. There will be about 1,000 workers in the nest by then, all working for the one queen that started the colony. When it is time, the queen starts to lay a different kind of egg, and the workers give the grubs a different diet. These grubs develop into ants with wings, both males and females. These new female ants will become queens. They crawl out of the nest and the **cycle** starts again.

Workers on a Production Line

Ants and honeybees have very similar societies. Among honeybees, each worker moves from one job to another according to a timetable. For the first three days of her adult life, a worker bee cleans out the wax cells in which the queen lays her eggs. Then **glands** on the worker bee's head start to produce special royal jelly, and she becomes a nursemaid. She feeds the larvae, which develop from the queen's eggs, a royal jelly for the first few days of their development. After this, most larvae are fed a mixture of pollen and honey. Only the larvae that are going to grow into new queen bees continue to be fed royal jelly throughout their lives.

When a worker is about 10 days old, her nurse glands stop making royal jelly, and glands on her **abdomen** start producing wax. She now does construction work, building new cells on the honeycomb and repairing damage to existing cells. On her 18th day, the worker bee starts to fly outside the hive, learning landmarks and finding her way around. She may also guard the hive and check incoming bees to make sure they are members of that hive.

Finally, at 21 days old, she becomes a forager, gathering pollen and nectar, which are food for the hive. Two or three weeks later, she dies, and the young workers responsible for keeping the hive clean take her body out and dump it.

From left to right are the different members of a honeybee colony: the queen bee, a drone (male), and a worker. A colony of bees has one queen, about 100 drones, and about 50,000 workers.

A honeybee queen (marked red) and workers. To the right of the queen are a few larvae in their cells. After 12 days, larvae emerge as full-grown workers.

The timetable is not absolutely fixed. Workers explore the hive and can change their behavior according to what needs to be done. If there is not enough food, they become foragers. If there are not enough young workers to look after the larvae, foragers go back to nursemaid duty, and their head glands start making royal jelly again.

When a hive gets full, the queen may move out with many of the workers to build a new hive at a different site. They swarm in one location until they are ready to build a hive. Scouts fly off in every direction to explore possible sites for a new hive.

Social Signals

A busy honeybee colony seems wonderfully organized, with each worker knowing exactly what to do. The bees give off chemicals that act as signals to tell each other what to do. Although the signals are simple, they can produce very complicated behavior. For example, when a bee dies, its body produces a particular chemical. If a scientist puts a drop of this chemical on a healthy, living worker bee, other workers will treat her as if she were dead. Even if she is clearly alive, they will pick her up and throw her out of the hive! They will even throw out the queen if she is dabbed with the same chemical.

A chemical signal even tells which bees are the members of a colony. Different colonies of the same kind of bee have slightly different smells. A worker bee learns the smell of her own colony as she is growing up. When she is on guard duty, she checks each incoming worker with her **antennae**. She attacks any that do not have her colony smell. Bees have other signals for when they are being attacked and when there is good food available.

The queen inspects cells. She may be preparing to lay eggs.

Where Did Insect Societies Come From?

Not all ants, wasps, and bees live in societies. For example, leaf-cutting bees live alone, caring for their young by themselves. Sometimes a group of sister wasps will share the job of building and protecting a mud nest, but each wasp looks after her own young.

Why and how did insect societies get started? There are two main ideas about how this happened. One idea is that some of the young female insects stayed in the nest to help their mother raise the next batch of offspring. The workers and the new offspring are sisters. By helping their mother, the workers may have more relatives than if they had laid their own eggs. As more eggs hatch, the nest becomes larger and social behavior becomes more common.

The other idea is that some female insects started sharing a nest. They might have been sisters, or they might have been unrelated. By working together instead of alone, they could build a nest more quickly and defend it better against attack. They could also protect one another's eggs from danger and gather more food. From that, a real society very likely started to develop.

Both theories are probably right. Some insects became social by staying at home to help, others by sharing a nest. Because these events took place long ago, we may never know exactly why insect societies began.

Worker bees have many roles. These two guard bees are killing an intruding wasp.

The bumble bee's nest might contain only a few hundred workers. It is much smaller than a honeybee hive.

13

4 / *Birds of a Feather*

"Birds of a feather flock together," says the proverb, and that is often true. Occasionally, however, small birds of different species may gather in a flock to find food. In the winter, when food is scarce, birds may be able to find better eating sites if they are part of an entire group of different birds searching together.

Kittiwakes breed in large colonies on steep cliffs where they are safe from enemies. They are found in Europe, Norway, Iceland, and the British Isles.

Waterfowl often gather together in a flock of mixed species. In this scene, the large white birds are mute swans, the small black birds are coots, and the rest are ducks.

A flock is usually made up of just one kind of bird, but a flock is not always a society. A flock is less complicated than a society of insects because the birds might not have division of labor. Birds generally are social because they receive help finding their food and avoiding **predators**. Some birds live in groups, and some birds work together in societies.

Safety in a Group

A goshawk out hunting will easily catch a pigeon that is by itself. But if there is a flock of 50 or more pigeons, the goshawk seldom ever catches one. In a large flock, one of the birds is sure to see the goshawk and fly away, and all the others will follow.

There are other benefits to being in a group. A flock of small birds can mob, or gang up on, a crow or a hawk until it gives up and goes away. A little bird on its own would not be able to drive away a predator. A predator also has difficulty hunting a bird in a large flock. For example, a falcon diving into a flock of starlings risks missing its target and injuring itself by hitting another bird.

Sea gulls often nest in very dense colonies and protect each other from hungry foxes in two ways. First, the huge number of birds keeps the foxes away, especially from the center of the colony. Second, the sea gulls all lay their eggs at the same time, so there will be more eggs and chicks than the foxes can steal. Although the foxes will steal many, they certainly will not get them all. If the gulls did not all breed at the same time, the foxes would probably take more young gulls each year.

The peregrine falcon lives in Europe, Asia, and North America. It is a fierce predator, but it does not defend itself when attacked by a flock of smaller birds.

This photograph shows where a goshawk has plucked the feathers from ring doves before eating them.

Exchanging Information

Finding food is an important reason for birds flocking together. Some African weaverbirds live in huge nests with more than a hundred birds. The communal nest is an information center. In the morning, the birds fly off in search of seeds. Some birds are lucky and find a lot of seeds. Other birds are not so lucky and go hungry. When all of the birds return to the nest at night, the hungry birds can tell that the other birds found food. The next morning, those hungry birds will follow the birds that found food.

Real Societies

Some kinds of birds live in real societies. Florida scrub jays live in societies in the scrubby woodlands of Florida.

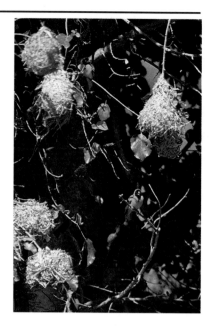

The black-headed weaverbird lives in central Africa. These birds weave their oval nests with great skill.

Social weavers of southwest Africa build communal nests. Each nesting pair has its own apartment. If you look carefully, you can see one or two heads peeping out from the nest.

Scrub jays live in pairs of male and female. Each pair has a **territory**. Many of the pairs have helpers, usually their young offspring born the year before. When the female lays eggs, those eggs must be protected from snakes and other predators. The helpers give warning calls and mob the predators. Chicks whose parents have a helper or two are more likely to survive than chicks whose parents do not have a helper. The helpers also bring food for the chicks.

Pairs of scrub jays with helpers can raise more chicks than pairs without helpers. The helpers would have their own chicks if they left the nest to find mates instead of staying to help their parents. However, most of the good territories are already taken by older scrub jays, so a young male would be very lucky to find an empty space. By staying at home, a young male has a chance to take over the territory when his father dies and then attract a female to share the territory. Young females help their parents until there is a male in a territory nearby with which to mate.

The Florida scrub jay lives in scrublands of oaks and pines in the southern parts of the United States. It builds a nest of twigs and stems in bushes about a yard (a meter) or so above the ground.

Nesting Together

The groove-billed ani, which lives in Texas, Central America, and South America, shares a communal nest. The birds form pairs, but three or four pairs often get together to build a communal nest. All the females lay their eggs in the nest, and all the members of the group take turns looking after the eggs and the chicks, protecting them from predators. But not all of the eggs will hatch.

Competition in the Nest

On the ground beneath the ani nest are the smashed remains of many eggs. Female anis all lay eggs, but the female ani of the dominant pair always begins to lay her eggs last. Before she lays her eggs, however, she rolls many of the other females' eggs out of the nest. The eggs fall to the ground and break. The other females will lay a few more eggs in the nest, but most that hatch will have been laid by the dominant female ani. In that way, the dominant pair produces more offspring.

A groove-billed ani at the communal nest. Several females lay eggs in the same nest, but many of the eggs are thrown out of the nest by the dominant female, who has not yet laid her eggs.

Once the eggs are laid, all of the anis protect them from predators. A flock is better than just two birds at defending a nest. The anis also take turns sitting on the eggs to incubate them so they will hatch.

Although scrub jays and groove-billed anis have societies which are more complicated than the average flock of birds, they do not really have division of labor. Helpers sometimes leave the scrub jay flock to mate and raise their own young.

In general, insect societies are complicated but strict—each worker does one job at a time and nothing else. With birds, and even more so with mammals, each animal does many different jobs, and those jobs may change frequently.

Anis live in the southern United States and in parts of Central America. They seem to have worked out a way of living together and surviving as a species.

5 | *Mammal Societies*

Mammals, like birds, often live in groups as a defense against predators. When prowling hyenas approach a herd of wildebeests, or gnu, a wildebeest cow will quietly lead her calf to a safer position on the far side of the herd. When wolves attack a herd of musk oxen, the bulls form a circle around the cows and calves and point their sharp horns toward the wolves. One musk ox on its own would be no match for a pack of wolves, but a whole herd can often keep the wolves away.

Animals hunting together catch more food. Hyenas hunting a wildebeest calf work in pairs or threesomes. One hyena distracts the mother while the others attack the calf. One hyena hunting alone would have a hard time taking a calf from its mother.

Two hyenas attack a wildebeest, or gnu, calf in Africa. By hunting in pairs or packs, hyenas can kill large animals.

Musk oxen form a defensive circle around a young calf. These hardy animals live in Greenland and northern Canada. During the Ice Age, musk oxen lived farther south, in Europe and Asia. Now there are not many herds left.

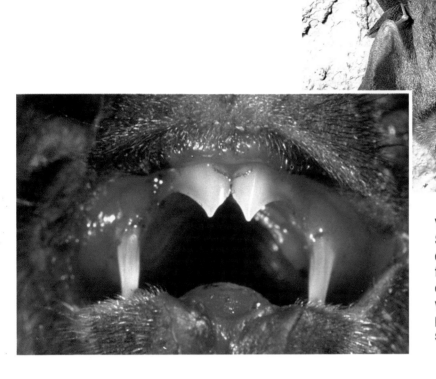

Vampire bats live in Mexico and South America. They can only digest blood, which they extract from other animals. The teeth of vampire bats are very sharp, which allows them to take blood painlessly, and undetected, from sleeping animals.

Friendly Vampires

There are many good reasons for living in a group. Vampire bats, which live in Mexico, Central America, and South America, tend to the mother of a newborn bat. Vampire bats drink blood, which they take from cattle and other livestock at night. A female bat that has just given birth cannot leave the roost to hunt, so the other bats will return after feeding and **regurgitate** some of the blood they drank. They feed it to the mother bat.

Later, when a young vampire bat is old enough, its mother will resume her nightly hunts for blood. She will return to the roost and regurgitate blood for her offspring to drink. When the young bat is able to tag along on a hunt, its mother may let it drink from a wound that she has opened on the livestock animal.

Eventually, the young bat will learn to hunt for itself, finding its own food sources. Vampire bats have been known to take blood from humans.

Mongoose Packs

The dwarf mongoose is a little animal that lives in old termite mounds in East Africa. One scientist who spent 15 years watching them thinks they are more sociable than any other animal, aside from people. Each pack is made up of about 15 mongooses. Only one pair—usually the oldest—breeds. All the others help the breeders look after the young.

A few mongooses stay behind at the den to guard the pups while the others are out looking for food. The mongooses take turns baby-sitting during the day, so each one gets a chance to hunt. When the pups are old enough to go out hunting, pack members dig up insects and let the young practice catching them.

Birds of prey try to capture mongooses, but they do not often succeed. One mongoose—usually a male—stands guard while the others are playing, looking for food, or grooming. As with baby-sitting, the mongooses take turns at guard duty. If one mongoose does get snatched up by a hawk, the others will try to rescue it.

The best helpers in a pack of dwarf mongooses are not related to the breeding adults. Often the helpers have come from another pack. They might be helping a lot so the other mongooses in the pack will let them stay.

A dwarf mongoose stands on guard to protect the pack from enemies. This is the smallest of the mongoose species.

A pack of dwarf mongooses outside their den. These little animals feed by day and shelter at night in burrows.

The Family That Preys Together

Almost all kinds of cats live alone. Even the male and female do not stay together after mating. The one exception is the lion, which has a very interesting social life.

Lions live in groups called prides, and at the heart of the pride are the females. They are all related: mothers, daughters, aunts, and cousins. Females usually stay in the pride when they grow up. The females usually work together to hunt for food and will help each other raise lion cubs.

Young males leave the pride, often kicked out by the adult males. They wander across the **savanna** together until they find a pride in which the adult males are getting old and weak. The young males challenge the old males to a fight, which can be very bloody. Sooner or later the old males are beaten, and the new lions take over the pride.

One of the first things the young males do is kill or chase away all of the young cubs. Killing the cubs seems brutal, but the new males want to have cubs of their own right away. A female who has had cubs will not be ready to have more until her cubs are two years old. If the female's young cubs have died, however, she is ready to breed again. The males want to have many cubs during the three or four years before they are challenged by a new group of young males.

Four lion cubs peer out from their lair in the Kenya scrubland. The lion is one of the big cats, which include tigers, jaguars, and leopards.

Several lionesses drink at a pool of stagnant water. In the African savanna, water is scarce during the dry season, which presents a problem for all large animals.

When all the cubs are dead, the lionesses are all ready to breed at the same time. More cubs will survive to adulthood if several litters are born at about the same time. A lioness raising cubs by herself has difficulty protecting her young while hunting.

When a pride of lionesses raises its cubs together, all the mothers look after the cubs and feed them. A lioness will even let another lioness's cubs compete with her own cubs for her milk. If a lioness dies or disappears, another lioness will adopt the missing lioness's cubs.

When the lionesses go out hunting, one or two will usually stay behind to take care of the cubs. The more lionesses there are with cubs and milk, the more helpers there are to look after the cubs.

As the cubs grow up, they have many brothers, sisters, and cousins of the same age. When the young males are kicked out of the pride, they all go together, and a bigger bunch stands a better chance of defeating the old males of another pride.

A large pride of lions rest in the savanna. This pride includes seven cubs, three adult females, and one adult male (background). There may be more lions who have left the pride for a short time, perhaps to get food or water.

Hunting

Living in a pride makes hunting easier and more successful. Several females working together can catch prey more easily than one lioness hunting on her own. Also, several lionesses can catch much larger animals, enough to feed the whole pride. The lionesses that stay behind to look after the cubs get a share, and so do any females too old or too sick to hunt.

A large pride is better able to defend its catch against a pack of hyenas that might try to take it from a single lion.

Two lionesses and some cubs eat their share of the kill after the lions have satisfied their appetites.

Eight lionesses gang up on a buffalo. The buffalo may soon lose its battle under this combined attack.

What about the males? The lionesses do the work, but when they have caught an animal, the males rush over and push them aside. The lionesses get to eat only after the lions have had their fill. The males steal the biggest portion, but they do little to earn it, aside from defending their territory from other males.

Scientists don't really know why lions are social. Perhaps it is to catch more food. That is why one scientist who has studied lions says, "The family that preys together, stays together."

6 / Primates

Of all the mammals, the **primates**—monkeys and apes—are the most social. Almost all primates live in groups of some sort.

Some, like the gibbons of Asia, live in small families: mother, father, and their young. Others, like the gelada baboons that live in Ethiopia, gather in bands of a thousand or more. But very few primates live on their own.

The exceptions are the nocturnal primates, who sleep during the day and come out at night. Most nocturnal primates live alone. When danger threatens, they hide, rather than attacking or running away. An animal on its own can hide better than a whole group.

A white-handed gibbon of southeast Asia. Its long arms help it swing easily from one tree to another.

A bush baby, or galago, photographed at night. These nocturnal animals come from Africa. They have tails that are longer than their bodies.

Marmosets live in the jungle of eastern Brazil, near the mouth of the Amazon River. Their bushy tails are one and a half times their body length. Their fur is very soft, and they have white tufts of fur on their ears.

There are many kinds of societies among the primates. Some primates live solitary lives, coming together with others of their species only to breed. The females will raise their offspring alone. Eventually, the young will leave their mothers to live by themselves.

Only a few primates live in simple families of mother, father, and their young. Gibbons have simple families, and so do the marmosets of South America. In marmoset families, the female usually gives birth to twins. The male helps her by carrying the two youngsters through the treetops. If the male dies, the female often leaves her twins behind and goes on without them.

Among primates, societies in which there are more females than males are much more common than simple families. The female primates allow one male to stay with them. We call these "one-male units."

Baboons of Ethiopia

Two kinds of baboon, the hamadryas baboon and the gelada baboon, live in one-male units. One male stays with several females and chases away any other males that try to come near the females. But hamadryas and gelada baboon societies are very different.

Among hamadryas baboons, young females leave their mothers and follow a male. The male tries to control the females in his group, biting them on the neck if they should stray. He also tries to keep all other males away. The females in a hamadryas unit do what the male wants them to do. The big male, with his dramatic fur mane, is the center of the society.

Young female gelada baboons stay with their mothers. All the females in the unit know one another, and they are probably related. They allow one male to join them. The male tries to keep other males away, but he is often unsuccessful. The females decide where to go and what to do, and the male has to tag along.

A hamadryas, or sacred, baboon on a tree branch with its baby. These baboons are found in Somalia, which is on the northeast coast of Africa, and near the Red Sea.

A troop of hamadryas baboons, including an old male with his silvery mane and two baby baboons, perch on a rock.

On the average, in hamadryas and gelada societies, one male might have about 10 females in a unit. Males who do not have any females live with a unit of other males who also do not have females. Several units travel together as a troop, and troops often share a safe sleeping site, perhaps on a cliff.

Mountain gorillas live in the forests of Zaire and central Africa. They are very strong but will not attack unless angered. This is a female with her young.

Ape Societies

There are three kinds of great ape: the chimpanzee, the gorilla, and the orangutan, each with a different kind of society. Orangutans are solitary. Females wander through the rain forest with their youngest offspring, searching for trees that have ripe fruit. They do not form pairs of males and females.

Chimpanzee society changes all the time. Mothers and their young stay together, but different families come together as a group and then split up. Two mothers might travel together for a few days, then join several other families at a ripe fig tree. When the figs are eaten, the families might go off on their own or together in different groups. Males will eventually leave their mothers and form shifting groups that join and split.

Gorillas are more settled. One male, called a silverback because of the gray hair on his back, gathers a group of females around him. The females come from several different groups, and the silverback protects them against enemies and keeps other male gorillas away.

People are primates, too, and our closest relatives are chimpanzees and gorillas. But we live in many different kinds of societies.

Chimpanzees are the most intelligent of the primates and have been very closely studied by scientists.

Glossary

abdomen: the hind part of an insect's body. In mammals, the abdomen is the belly.

antennae: feelers projecting from the head of an insect and from some water animals.

colony: a group of animals or plants of the same kind, that lives or grows together.

cycle: a chain of events that occurs in the same order, over and over again.

gland: an organ that makes a substance, which can then be used in or outside of the body.

larvae: insects that have just been hatched and look like tiny worms. They will change to look like their parents as they get older.

paralyze: to be without feeling and unable to move.

predator: any animal that hunts and eats other animals. Lions are predators.

primate: a group of mammals that includes apes, monkeys, and humans.

regurgitate: to bring undigested food up from the stomach to the mouth.

savanna: a hot, dry grassland with few trees.

species: a class of animals or plants that look alike. Members of one species cannot usually breed with those of another species.

tentacle: a long, flexible arm or leg that some animals have for feeling and gripping. An octopus has eight tentacles.

territory: an area of land in which an animal or group of animals lives. Animals mark out and protect their territories.

Index

Pages shown in *italic* type include pictures of the animals.

ani, groove-billed, *18-19*
ants, 9, *10*, 11
apes, 26, *29-30*
aphids, 9, *10*

baboons, 4-6, 28-29
    gelada, 28-29
    hamadryas, *28-29*
    olive, *4-6*
black-spotted grunt, *4*
buffalo, *25*
bumble bee, *13*
bush baby, *26*

chimpanzee, 29-*30*
communal nest, 17, 19
coral, *7*

division of labor, 8
duck, *14*

falcon, *15*
fish, 4
Florida scrub jay, 16-*17*
fox, 15

gibbon, *26*, 27
gnu, *See* wildebeest

gorilla, *29*-30
goshawk, *15*

honeybee, 9, *11-12*, *13*
hyenas, *20*

kittiwakes, *14*

leaf-cutting bees, 13
leopard, *5*
lion, *23-25*

marmoset, *27*
mongoose, dwarf, *22*

musk oxen, *20*
mute swans, *14*

one-male unit,
    among primates, 27
orangutan, 29

pigeon, 15
Portuguese man-of-war, *8*

sea gulls, 15

Shetland ponies, *3*
snow geese, *3*
social traits, 9
social weavers, *16*
society, *definition of*, 4
starlings, 15

termites, *9*
tropical reefs, 7

vampire bats, *21*

wasps, 9, *13*
weaverbirds, *16*
wildebeest, *20*
wolf, 20

Library of Congress Cataloging-In-Publication Data

Cherfas, Jeremy.
    Animal societies / Jeremy Cherfas.
        p.   cm.—(How animals behave)
    Includes index.
    Summary: Describes the complex and varied ways
animals, from termites to migrating birds, interact and
behave in groups.
    ISBN 0-8225-2254-3: $10.95
    1. Animal societies—Juvenile literature. |1. Animal
    societies.|
I. Title. II. Series: Cherfas, Jeremy. How animals behave.
QL775.C515   1991
591.52'46—dc20   90-44253
                                       CIP
                                        AC

Acknowledgments
The publishers wish to thank the following photographers
and agencies whose photographs appear in this book. The
photographs are credited below by page number and position on the page (B—Bottom, T—Top, L—Left, and
R—Right):

Ardea London Ltd: 13B, 16T, Clem Haagner 5T, Valerie
Taylor 7T, John Mason 8B, 11B, Richard Vaughan 12T,
Francois Gohier 20B, Adrian Warren 21R, Arthus-Bertrand
23B. Bruce Coleman Ltd: Frans Lanting 3T, Peter Davey 6,
Frieder Sauer 7B, Jane Burton 9T, 26B, Kim Taylor 10T,
Jan Taylor 10B, H.J. Flugel 13T, R. Wilmshurst 14R,
Dr. Eckart Pott 14L, 15B, Hans Reinhard 15T, Francisco
Erice 16B, Gunter Ziesler 18, 21L, 22T, 23T, K. Wothe
19, Norman Tomalin 26T, Rod Willaims 27, Francisco Futil
28B, R.I.M. Campbell 29. Eric and David Hosking: 5B,
D.P. Wilson 8T. Frank Lane Picture Agency: Silvestris
4R, B. Borrell 9B, Treat Davidson 11T, 12B, Peter Davey
20T, 25R, Fritz Polking 28T. NHPA: R.J. Erwin 17. Nature
Photographers Ltd: Andrew Cleave 3B, Don Smith 4L,
Hugo van Lawick 22B, Roger Tidman 24, 25L, Kevin
Carlson 30.
Front cover photograph: Kenneth Lorenzen, University of
California, Davis.

Editorial planning by Jollands Editions
Designed by Alison Anholt-White
Color origination by Golden Cup Printing Co., Ltd,
    Hong Kong
Printed in Great Britain by Eagle Colourbooks Ltd.

Bound in the United States of America